This book belongs to:

A is for ANGRY

A is for

angry animals advancing alor

by Sandra Boynton

Library of Congress Cataloging-in-Publication Data

Boynton, Sandra.
A is for angry.

Summary: A big bashful bear, a cute clean cat, and
other alliteratively described animals introduce the
letters of the alphabet.
1. English language—Alphabet.   2. English
language—Adjective.   [1. Alphabet.   2. English language
—Adjective]   I. Title
PE1155.B64   1983   83-40038.
ISBN-13: 978-0-89480-507-3

Design by Sandra Boynton and Paul Hanson

*Workman books are available at special discounts
when purchased in bulk for premiums and sales
promotions as well as for fund-raising or
educational use. Special editions or book excerpts can
also be created to specification. For details,
contact the Special Sales Director at the address below.*

Workman Publishing Company, Inc.
225 Varick Street
New York, NY 10014-4381
www.workman.com

First printing October 1983

15   14

is for **PAM**
and so is this book

ant

anteater

is for **ANGRY**

bear

is for BASHFUL

 bunny

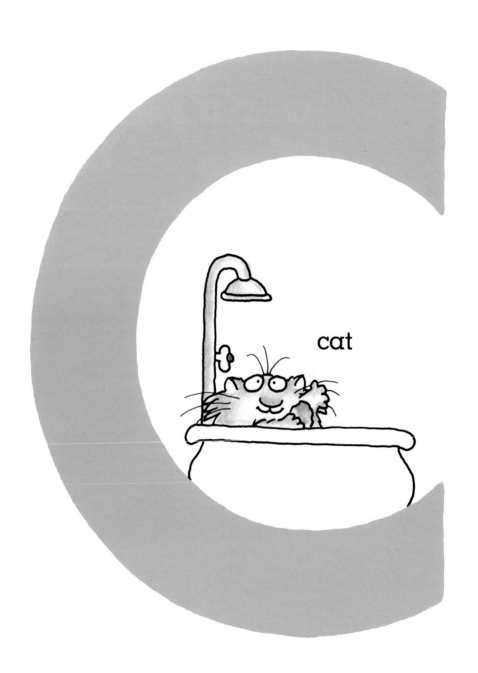

cat

is for CLEAN

ogs

is for **DIRTY**

is for **ENERGETIC**

elephant

lying fish

fox

is for **FRIGHTENED**

gorilla

s for **GRUMPY**

hippopotamus

is for HUNGRY

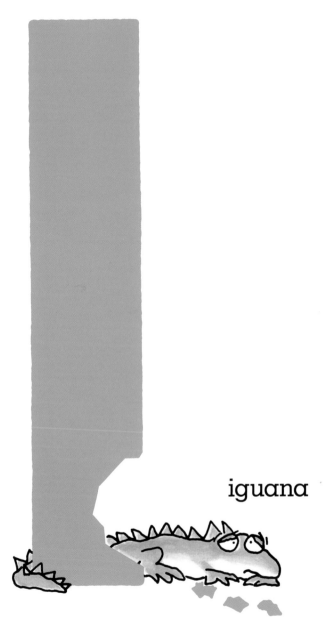

iguana

is for ILL

jaguar

is for JAZZY

koalas

is for **KIND**

is for

lion

OUD!

lambs

mice

is for MERRY

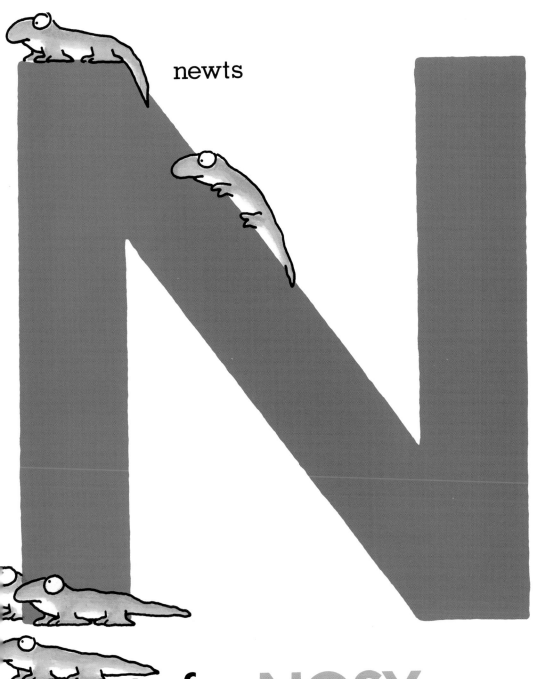

newts

is for NOSY

opossum

is for **OUTRAGED**

pig

is for **PLAYFUL**

quail

is for QUICK

rhinoceros

is for ROTUND

snake

is for SLEEPY

turkey

turkey trap

is for TANGLED

is for UPSIDE-DOWN

unau

vulture

is for **VAIN**

walrus

is for WIDE

isn't for anything

yak

is for YOUNG

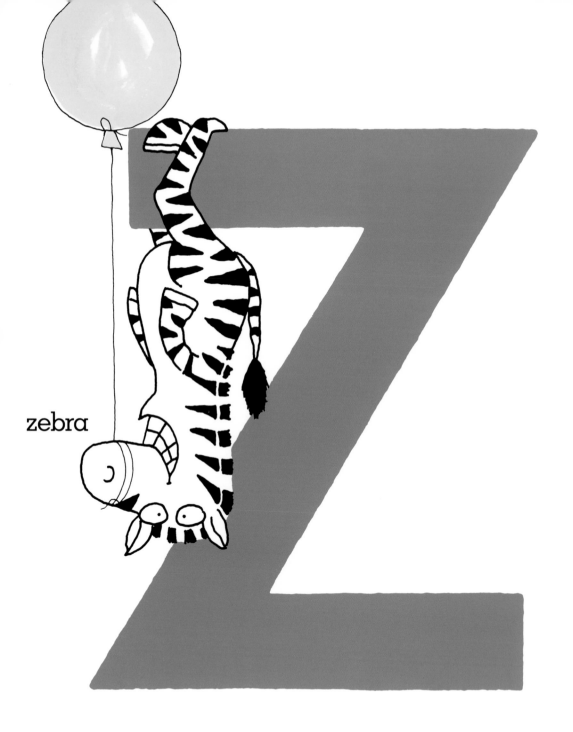

zebra

is for ZANY

and

is for

And Z is for ZZZZZ

ZZZZZZZZZZZZ.